Text © 1996 Walker Books Ltd
Illustrations © 1994, 1996 Anita Jeram
Based on the book *Guess How Much I Love You*™
written by Sam McBratney

This edition published 1997 by Walker Books Ltd
87 Vauxhall Walk
London SE11 5HJ

10 9

Printed in Italy

ISBN 0-7445-6118-3

MY BABY BOOK

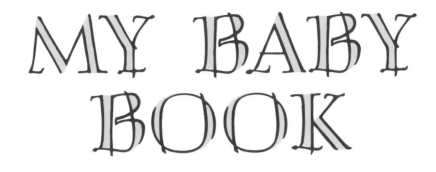

illustrated by
Anita Jeram

— Based on —

GUESS HOW MUCH
I LOVE YOU™

written by
Sam McBratney

MY FAMILY

Before there was me,
there was the rest of my family...

My mum: _____

Her birth date: _____

My dad: _____

His birth date: _____

The names and birth dates of other

people in my family:

_____

_____

_____

_____

Here are some pictures of my family.

Place pictures here

Guess how much I love them all.
And guess how much
they love me!

MY FIRST NINE MONTHS

Mum and Dad first found out they were expecting me in the month of _____ .

The name of Mum's doctor was _____ .

Mum thought I would be a

girl ☐   boy ☐

Dad thought I would be a

girl ☐   boy ☐

Here are some of the names they thought of for me if I was a girl _____

_____

and if I was a boy _____

_____

_____ .

The name they finally chose for me was

_____ .

*Guess how much
I love it!*

9

Here is a picture of Mum when she was expecting me.

Place picture here

While she was expecting me, Mum liked
these foods _____

_____ ,

but she didn't like these foods _____

_____ .

Some of the ways Mum and Dad got ready for

my arrival were _____

_____

_____ .

The date they first heard my heartbeat

was _____ .

The date they first felt me kick

was _____ .

The date I was due to be born

was _____ .

*Guess how excited we all were as
that date came closer.
Soon we would all meet!*

BEING BORN

 *At last, I was born!*

The date I arrived was

_____ .

So now that's my birthday!

The place was

_____

_____

_____

_____ .

When I was born it was

night ☐   day ☐

The time was

_____ .

ME

Here is the first picture of me ever!

Place picture here

Guess what I was like when I was born!

I weighed _____ . I measured _____ .

The colour of my eyes was _____ .

The colour of my hair was _____ .

Mum said I looked like _____ .

Dad said I looked like _____ .

Other people said I looked like _____

_____

_____ .

Guess who I think
I looked like?
ME!

FIRST DAYS

Mum and Dad told everyone about me!

Some first gifts I was given were

_____

_____

_____ .

The first car I

ever rode in was a

_____ .

*Guess how sleepy
I was when I was new!*

My first home was at

_____

_____

_____ .

Here are the autographs of some of the first

people I ever met: _____

_____

_____

_____

The first song that was ever sung to me

was _____ .

Guess how much I loved it!

 KEEPSAKES

My newspaper announcement

My hospital bracelet

My birth announcement card

MY FIRST FOOTPRINTS

Here are my baby footprints. Aren't they tiny?

Guess how much everyone loved me.

All the way up to my toes!

OTHER NEWS

*Guess what other things were going on
in the world when I was born.*

The Prime Minister was _____ .

Other leaders around the world were _____

_____ .

The clothes in fashion were _____

_____ .

Some hit songs were _____

_____ .

Some famous film stars were _____

_____ .

Some famous athletes were

_____

_____

_____ .

Here is a picture of me, after my first week in the world!

Place picture here

A newspaper cost _____ , a cinema ticket

cost _____ and a carton of milk cost _____ .

A postage stamp

looked like this:

FIRST BABY FEATS

I first slept through the night when

I was _____ old.

I first smiled when

I was _____ old.

I first discovered my hands when

I was _____ old.

I first grasped something when

I was _____ old.

I first discovered my feet when

I was _____ old.

I first clapped when

I was _____ old.

I first waved bye-bye when

I was _____ old.

Guess how much I loved being tickled!

EATING

The first solid food I ever tasted

was _____ .

I cut my first tooth on _____ .

I cut my second tooth on _____ .

I cut my third tooth on _____ .

I cut my fourth tooth on _____ .

I first drank from a cup when

I was _____ old.

I first used a spoon when

I was _____ old.

Guess what my favourite things to eat

were: _____

_____

_____

Yum!

Guess what my least favourite things to eat

were: _____

_____

_____

Yuck!

UP AND ABOUT

I first held my head up when

I was _____ old.

I first rolled over when

I was _____ old.

I first sat up alone when

I was _____ old.

I first crawled when

I was _____ old.

I could pull up to standing when

I was _____ old.

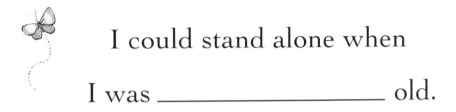

I could stand alone when

I was _____ old.

At last! I took my first step when

I was _____ old.

Guess how often I fell over! Oops-a-daisy!

TALKING

My first word *ever* was

_____ .

My first name for Mum was _____
and my first name for Dad was _____ .

Some of my other first words

were _____

_____ .

My favourite rhymes to say

were _____

_____ .

My favourite songs to sing

were _____

_____

_____ .

Guess how much I loved talking!

PLAYING

My first friends were _____

_____ .

My favourite toys were _____

_____ .

My favourite things to

do outside were

_____

_____

_____

_____ .

My favourite bedtime books were _____

_____ .

CHRISTMAS

People I celebrated my first Christmas with were

_____

_____

_____ .

Presents I was given were _____

_____

_____ .

Happy things that

happened were

_____

_____

_____

_____ .

BUMPS AND BRUISES

Sometimes I got ill, or hurt myself.

Some first illnesses I had

were _____

_____

_____ .

My doctor's name was

_____ .

Some baby medicines I had to take

were

 .

Some illnesses I was immunized against

were _____

_____

_____ .

Some bumps and falls I had

were _____

_____

_____ .

*Guess how much I liked
being kissed better!*

ON HOLIDAY

The first holiday I ever went on with my

family was to _____ ,

when I was _____ old.

Some adventures we had

were _____

_____

_____

_____ .

Here are some pictures of us on holiday.

Place pictures here

Guess how much I love holidays!
Across the river and over the hills!

MY FIRST BIRTHDAY

*Happy hoppy
birthday!*

People who sang "Happy Birthday"

to me that day were _____

_____ .

Special birthday things we ate

were _____ .

Some presents I was given were _____

_____

_____ .

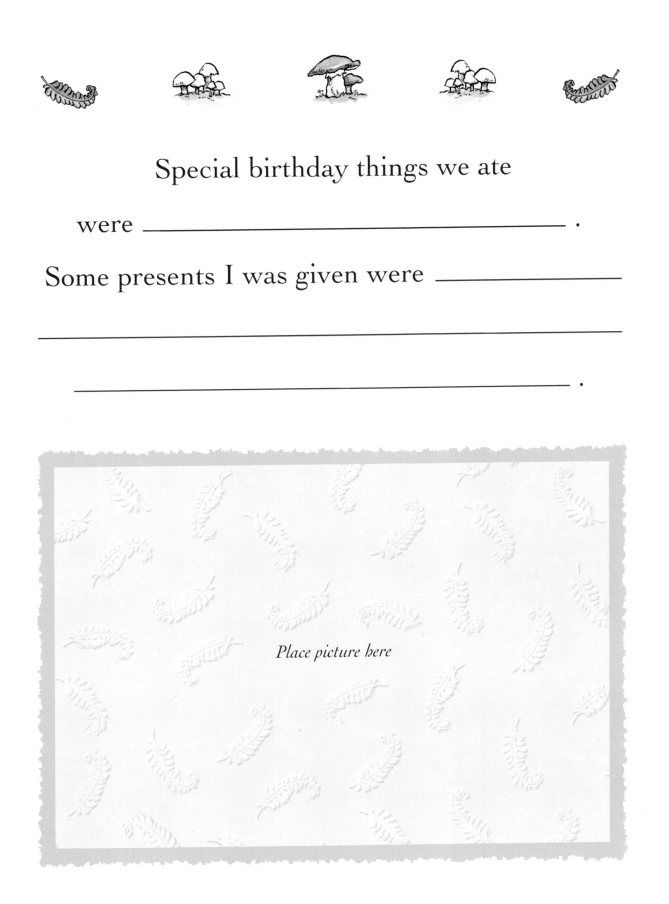

Place picture here

Here I am aged exactly one!

MY SECOND BIRTHDAY

Here I am aged exactly two!

Place picture here

Some presents I was given that day were

_____ .

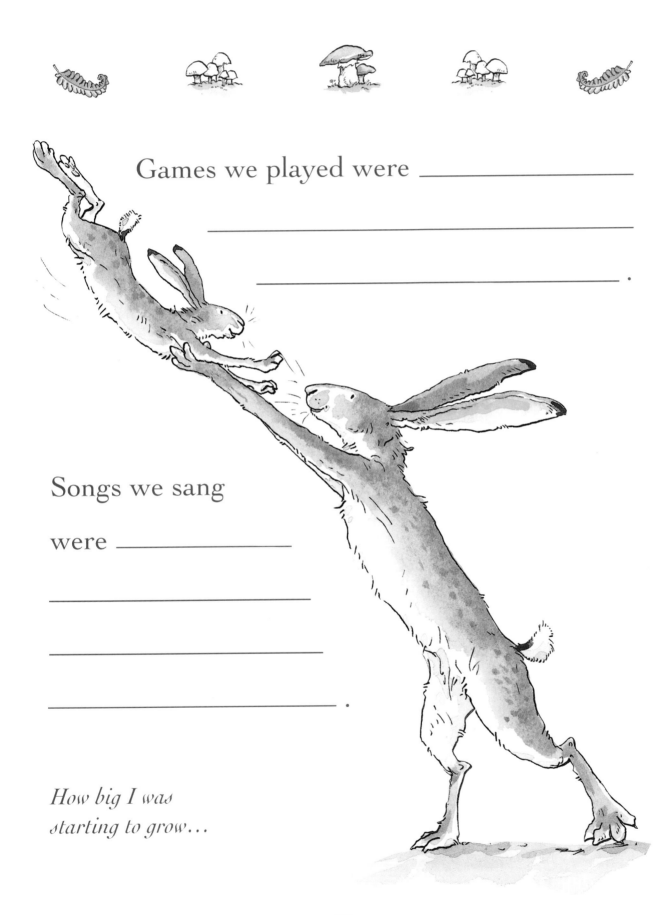

Games we played were _____

_____

_____ .

Songs we sang

were _____

_____

_____

_____ .

How big I was
starting to grow…

GROWING

I grew and grew – I couldn't stop!

Date	Age	Height	Weight
_____	_____	_____	_____
_____	_____	_____	_____
_____	_____	_____	_____
_____	_____	_____	_____
_____	_____	_____	_____
_____	_____	_____	_____
_____	_____	_____	_____
_____	_____	_____	_____
_____	_____	_____	_____
_____	_____	_____	_____

I could never have done it without my family!
They helped me all the way…

*Guess how much I love them —
right up to the MOON!*

*And guess how much
they love me—right up to the
moon AND BACK!*

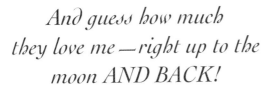

SPECIAL MEMORIES

Here are some special pictures and memories …

of other things we did when I was small…

*Guess how much
I'll treasure
them …*

*one day when
I've grown
tall!*